Dear Parents,

Welcome to the Scholastic Reader series. We have taken over 80 years of experience with teachers, parents, and children and put it into a program that is designed to match your child's interests and skills.

Level 1—Short sentences and stories made up of words kids can sound out using their phonics skills and words that are important to remember.

Level 2—Longer sentences and stories with words kids need to know and new "big" words that they will want to know.

Level 3—From sentences to paragraphs to longer stories, these books have large "chunks" of texts and are made up of a rich vocabulary.

Level 4—First chapter books with more words and fewer pictures.

It is important that children learn to read well enough to succeed in school and beyond. Here are ideas for reading this book with your child:

- Look at the book together. Encourage your child to read the title and make a prediction about the story.
- Read the book together. Encourage your child to sound out words when appropriate. When your child struggles, you can help by providing the word.
- Encourage your child to retell the story. This is a great way to check for comprehension.
- Have your child take the fluency test on the last page to check progress.

Scholastic Readers are designed to support your child's efforts to learn how to read at every age and every stage. Enjoy helping your child learn to read and love to read.

—**Francie Alexander**
Chief Education Officer
Scholastic Education

For Brad, my drawing pal.
—M.R.

3 3113 02269 0020

Copyright © 2003 by Michael Rex.
All rights reserved. Published by Scholastic Inc.
SCHOLASTIC, WORD BY WORD FIRST READER, CARTWHEEL BOOKS, and associated logos are trademarks and/or registered trademarks of Scholastic Inc.

Library of Congress Cataloging-in-Publication Data
Rex, Michael.
  Pals / by Michael Rex.
    p. cm. — (Word by word first reader)
Summary: An alien visits a house on Earth, where he meets a young boy and shares drawings with him.
  ISBN 0-439-49310-2
  [1. Extraterrestrial beings—Fiction. 2. Drawing—Fiction. 3. Friendship—Fiction.]
I. Title. II. Series.
PZ7.R32875 Fr 2003
[E]—dc21
                                    2002014397

10 9 8 7 6 5 4 3 2 1   03 04 05 06 07
Printed in the U.S.A. 23 • First printing, May 2003

PALS

A WORD BY WORD FIRST READER

by Michael Rex

Cartwheel
·B·O·O·K·S· ®

SCHOLASTIC INC.

New York   Toronto   London   Auckland   Sydney
Mexico City   New Delhi   Hong Kong   Buenos Aires

Over.

Down.

Out.

Boy.

Look.

In.

Show.

Draw.

Show.

Smile.

Draw.

Show.

Laugh.

Draw.

Pet.

Pet.

Game.

Game.

School.

School.

House.

House.

Homesick.

Trade.

Good-bye.

Draw.

Pals.

◆ WORD LIST ◆

boy	look
down	out
draw	over
game	pals
good-bye	pet
homesick	school
house	show
in	smile
laugh	trade

Fluency Fun

The words in each list below end in the same sounds.
Read the words in a list.
Read them again.
Read them faster.
Try to read all 12 words in one minute.

bin	**get**	**came**
pin	**let**	**game**
win	**pet**	**name**
twin	**wet**	**same**

Look for these words in the story.

over	**down**	**out**
look	**school**